The Land Before Time: Saro Tells a Story
© 2007 Universal Studios Licensing LLLP. The Land Before Time and related characters are trademarks and copyrights
of Universal Studios and U-Drive Productions, Inc. Licensed by Universal Studios Licensing LLLP. All rights reserved.
Printed in the United States of America.
All rights reserved. No part of this book may be used or reproduced in any manner whatsoever
without written permission except in the case of brief quotations embodied in critical articles and reviews.
For information address HarperCollins Children's Books, a division of HarperCollins Publishers,
1350 Avenue of the Americas, New York, NY 10019.
www.harpercollinschildrens.com

Library of Congress catalog card number: 2007928022
ISBN 978-0-06-134766-5
Typography by Rick Farley and Sean Boggs
❖
First Edition

THE LAND BEFORE TIME™

Saro Tells a Story

Based on the teleplay "The Legend of the Story Speaker" by Kent Redeker
Adapted by Jennifer Frantz
Illustrated by Charles Grosvenor and Artful Doodlers

HarperEntertainment
An Imprint of HarperCollinsPublishers

As Grandpa Longneck finished a story for Littlefoot and his friends, he looked up and said, "And *that* is how the Longnecks got their long necks."

"Wow!" Littlefoot said. "That was a great story, Grandpa!"

Just then, another Longneck stepped out from behind the bushes.

"I'm not so sure you're telling that story right," the voice said.

"Saro!" Grandpa Longneck shouted.

"Children, meet an old friend of mine," Grandpa Longneck said. "His name is Saro."

Saro looked at Littlefoot and his friends. "Did you know that your Grandpa was once a great Story Speaker?" he asked.

"What's a Story Speaker?" Cera asked.

"A Story Speaker travels the land telling great stories to all the Longneck herds," Saro said. "It is a very important job because it teaches the younger herds about their past."

"I like stories!" Chomper said.

"I do, too. I do! I do!" Ducky said.

"Some of the Longnecks have begun to forget their stories," Saro said sadly. "We need you to come back and be a Story Speaker again."

"I'm sorry, Saro," Grandpa said. "My days of wandering the land have passed. Now my place is here in the Great Valley with my family."

Saro became upset. "You have turned your back on the
Longnecks and their traditions," he said to Grandpa Longneck.
Then Saro walked off angrily through the bushes.
"Wait . . . " Grandpa Longneck shouted after him.
But Saro did not stop.

Littlefoot asked Grandpa if he was okay.

"I had hoped Saro would someday become a **Story Speaker** like me," Grandpa Longneck said. "He knows the stories well."

"Why didn't you tell him?" Littlefoot asked.

"I never had the chance," Grandpa Longneck said.

Suddenly Littlefoot had an idea! He would go find Saro for Grandpa Longneck. That way the Longneck stories would never be forgotten!

Littlefoot followed Saro's footsteps, which led to the
Mysterious Beyond. As he neared this new land, Littlefoot
tried to be brave, but he was scared and lonely.

Littlefoot heard a rustling sound in the bushes.
"Who . . . who is it?" he asked in a shaky voice.

It was Chomper! He had followed Littlefoot.

"Where are you going, Littlefoot?" Chomper asked.

"I'm following Saro's footprints. I have to find him for Grandpa!" Littlefoot said.

"Then you will need my help! With my sniffer, we will find him fast!" Chomper said.

Littlefoot was
happy to have a friend along.

Littlefoot helped
Chomper cross the river.

And Chomper helped Littlefoot climb a ledge.

In no time, the two friends caught up with Saro.

"Littlefoot! Chomper!" Saro said. "Why are you following me?" Before they could explain, the ground began to rumble. "Sliding rocks!" Chomper cried.

Rocks fell all around them, blocking the way back to the Great Valley. Littlefoot, Chomper, and Saro were trapped in the Mysterious Beyond!

"What are we going to do?" Chomper asked.

He and Littlefoot were very afraid.

Saro knew what to do. He began to tell Littlefoot and Chomper a story.

Once there was a Longneck named Tall Stepper.
One day, the Wind grew jealous and carried Tall Stepper's sister up to his Wind Cave in a tall, tall mountain.

Tall Stepper was afraid, but he had to help his sister.
So he challenged the Wind to a race down the mountain.
If Tall Stepper won, the Wind would release his sister.

The path down the mountain
was steep, and no one had
ever beaten the Wind.

But Tall Stepper was brave.
He found courage and was able to
beat the Wind down the mountain.

The Wind kept his promise,
and freed Tall Stepper's sister.

Saro looked at Littlefoot and Chomper. "When I need courage," he said. "I think of Tall Stepper."

"Thanks for telling us that story," Littlefoot said.

"I feel better now," Chomper added.

**Suddenly they heard voices. It was Grandpa Longneck,
Petrie, and the rest of their Longneck friends!**
   "Littlefoot!" Grandpa Longneck called.
   "Me find you!" Petrie cried from the sky.

Grandpa Longneck and the Longneck friends cleared the
rocks away. Littlefoot, Chomper, and Saro were saved!
   "Saro, there's something I want to talk to you about,"
Grandpa Longneck said. "*You* should be the new Story Speaker."
   "Me?" Saro asked. "But I can't tell the great stories without you."

"You told *us* a story—about Tall Stepper," Littlefoot said.

"Your story helped us feel a lot better!" Chomper added.

"You used one of the great stories to teach someone a lesson. That's what a Story Speaker does," Grandpa Longneck said.

Saro looked at the others. "I don't know what to say," he said.

"I thought Story Speakers always had something to say!" Littlefoot said with a giggle.

Then everyone gathered around, and the new Story Speaker began to tell a very special story.